Road Trips & Rainbow Trout

AMELIA BRESSEY CHAPMAN

Road Trips & Rainbow Trout
Copyright © 2022 by Amelia Bressey Chapman

All rights reserved. No part of this publication may be reproduced, distributed, or transmitted in any form or by any means, including photocopying, recording, or other electronic or mechanical methods, without the prior written permission of the author, except in the case of brief quotations embodied in critical reviews and certain other non-commercial uses permitted by copyright law.

Tellwell Talent
www.tellwell.ca

ISBN
978-0-2288-6252-9 (Paperback)

A big thank you to my parents for encouraging me to take art classes when I was younger, my awesome art teacher Ron Mulvey, all my friends and family who kept saying I should make a colouring book and a super big thank you to my friend Mason for helping me pay for half of the costs of publishing this book! Thank you everyone I love you all!

To Shelley Boyd for helping me with the Sinixt language piece, Michele A. Sam, Leanna Gravelle and Sophie Pierre for helping me connect with Ktunaxa language speakers, Lesley Garlow for connecting me with the Touchstones Nelson Museums resources and Jesse Halton for helping me connect with people and troubleshoot ideas. Thank you so much!

Donations
Every purchase of the book sends 2$ to each school
Salish School of Spokane
&
Yaqan Nukiy School

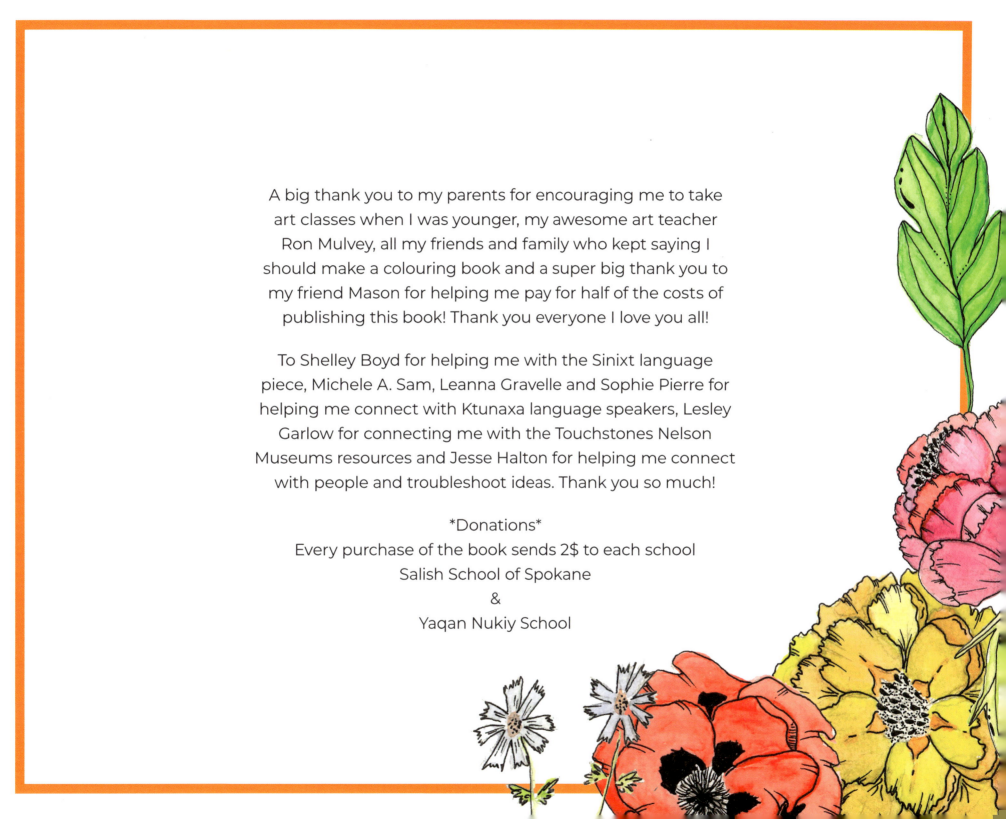

Musicians I listened to while drawing, I hope you'll enjoy them as much as I do!

John Muirhead

Snotty Nose Rez Kids

Cherry Street by The Icarus Account

Caamp

Kind of Yellow

Hey Ocean!

Stick With You by highasakite

Carmanah

Elisapie

Royal Canoe

The Oh Helios

Buffy Sainte Marie

Autumn Orange

Juniper Vale

Tycho

Studio Ghibli Soundtracks
Robin Guthrie
Delhi 2 Dublin
Home by Edward Sharpe / Magnetic O's
Walking On Sunshine by Katrina & The Waves
Aurora
Critical Role Podcast
Start Right Now feat Laney Jones by Young Pines
Heilung
Otyken
Clint Swanson
Moontricks
The Halluci Nation
Dead Can Dance

English - Killer Whale   sinixt - nx̌aʔx̌ʔitkʷ   ktunaxa - niɬxam'wuʔu

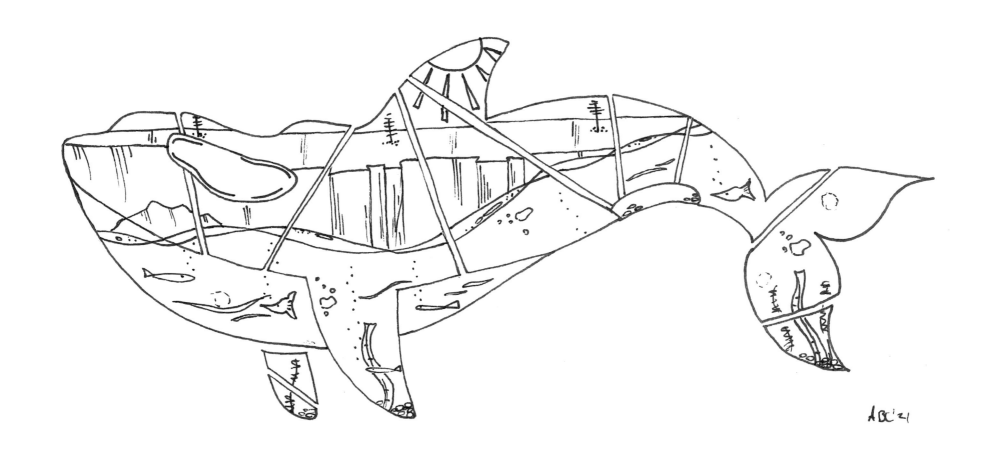

English - Deer   Sinixt - sk̓ʷak̓činm̓   ktunaxa - ȼupqa

English - Dandelion   ktunaxa - Ḱitq̓uɫ'katmaxaka

English - Mushroom   Ktunaxa ʔa·kaɬakaʔis watak

English - Salmon   Sinixt - ntytyix   ktunaxa - Swaɫmu

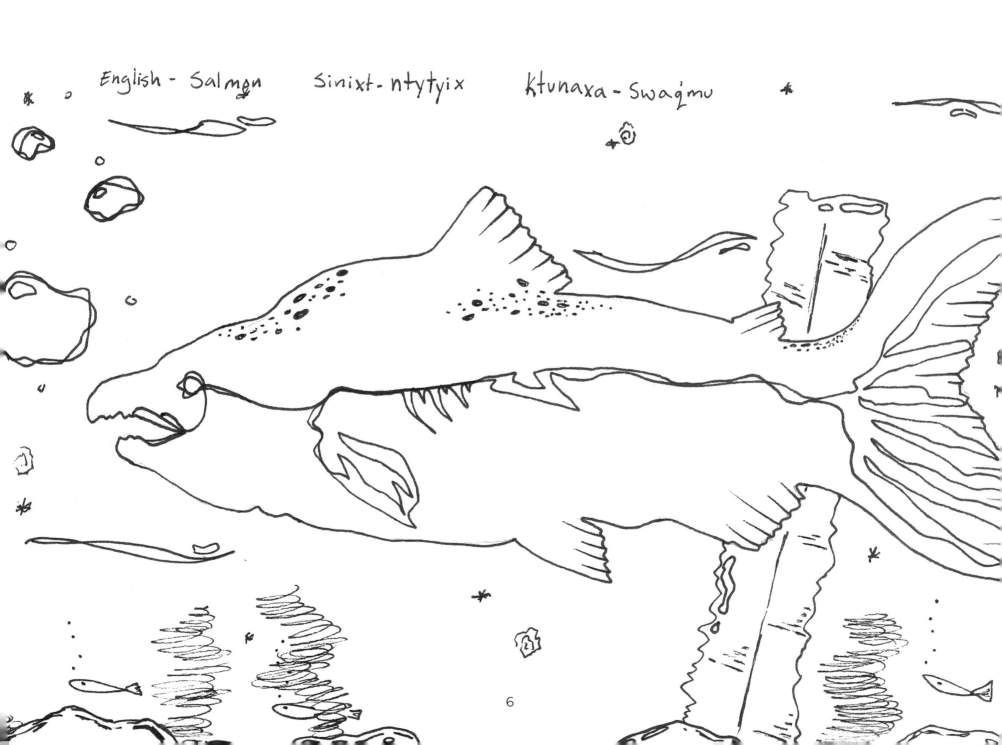

English - Skunk   Sinixt - Snkstiyaʔ   Ktunaxa - xaxas

English - *Beaver* Skull   Sinixt - šklaw̓   Ktunaxa - Sina

English - Frog　Sinixt- Sw̓ará k̓xn
ktunaxa - watak

English - Pond Lily   ktunaxa - ʔumk'ut

English - Indian Paintbrush   Ktunaxa - Kakaɬmukwatiɬik

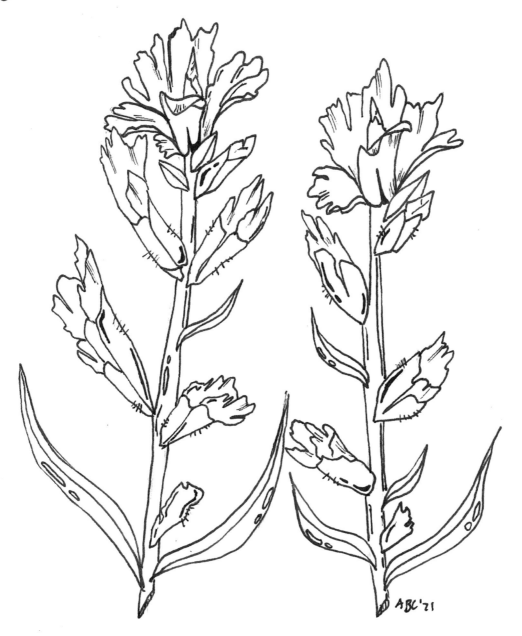

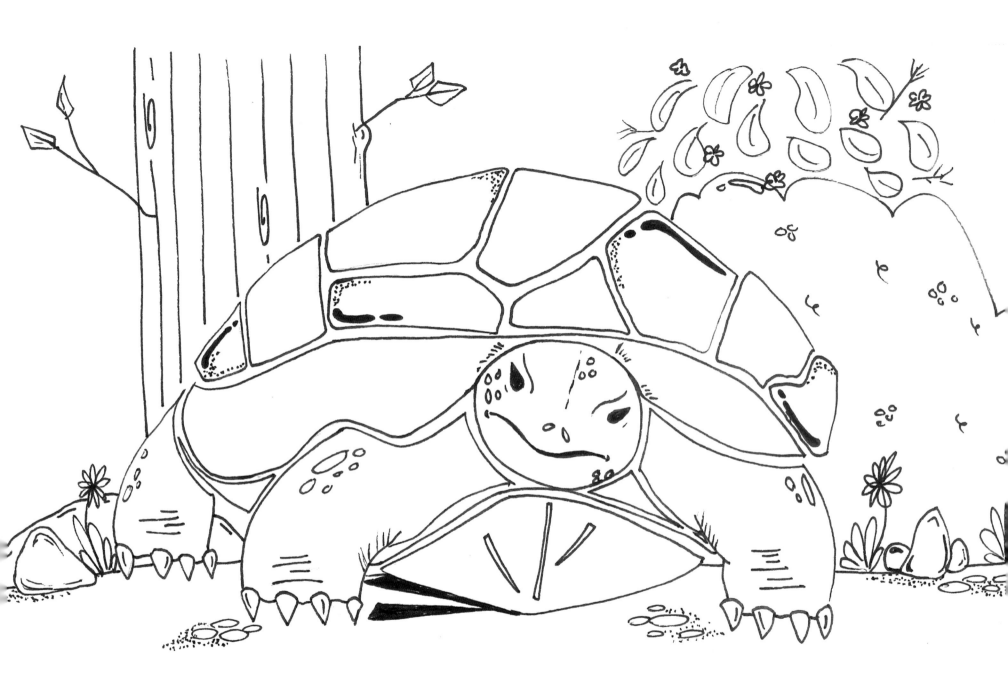

English - Turtle   Sinixt - parsikʷ   Ktunaxa - kaxax

English - Jellyfish

English - Barn *Owl*   Sinixt - Snina?   Ktunaxa - kupi

English - Camas   Sinixt - cx̌ʷlúsaʔ   Ktunaxa - xapi

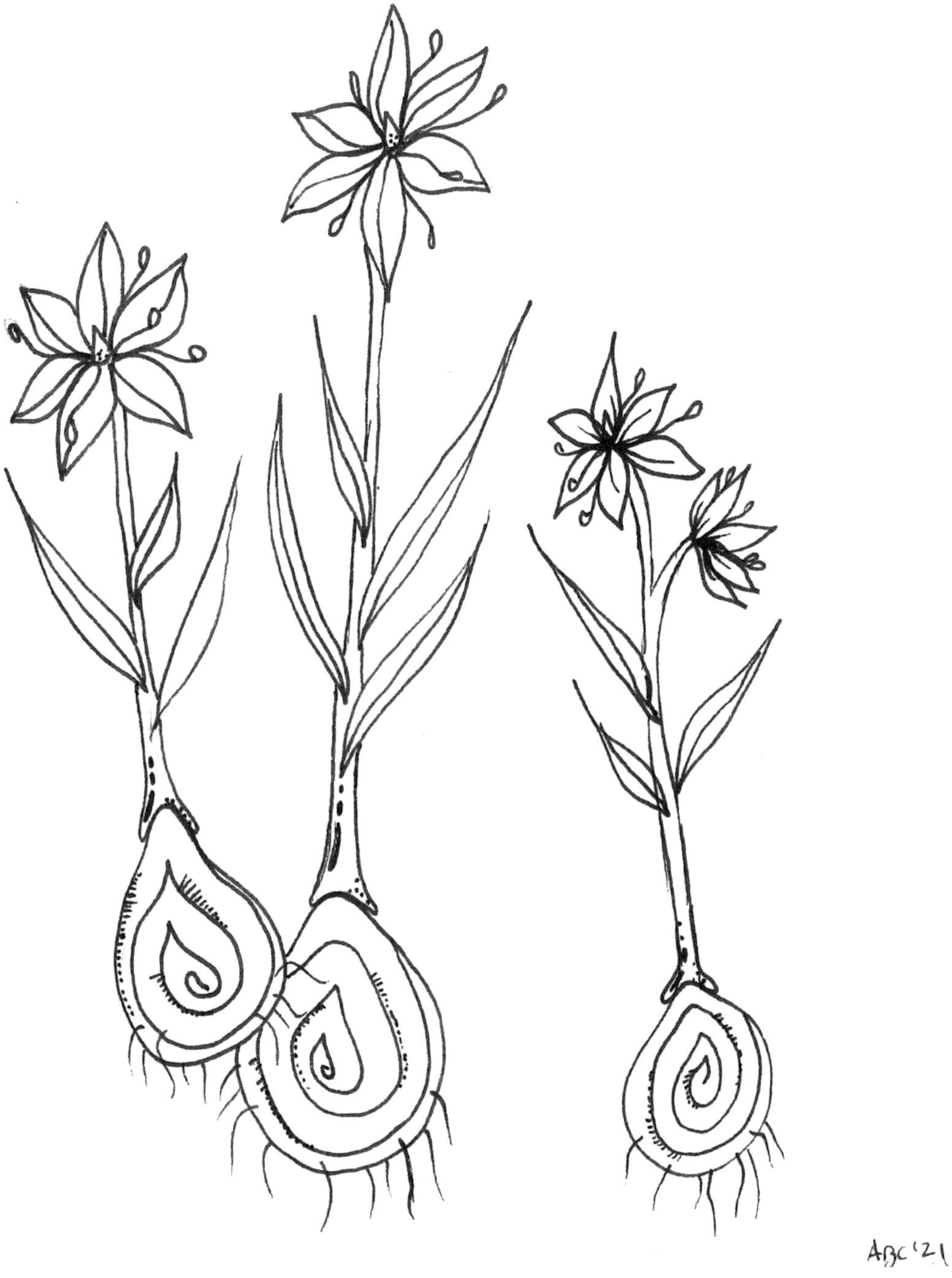

English - Rabbit   Sinixt - Spəpəlina?
Ktunaxa - kyanuqɬumna

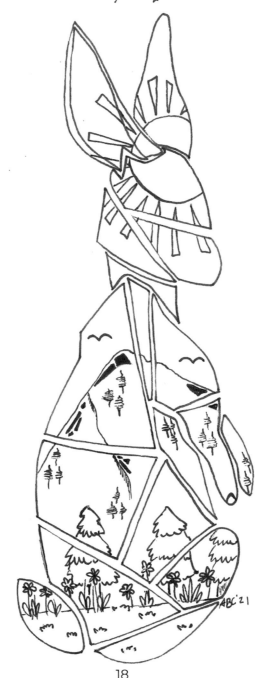

English - Wild Strawberries   Sinixt - tk'imtk'm
Ktunaxa - ʔa·q'uku

English - Chickadee • Ktunaxa - miɫ'qaqas

English - Bear   Sinixt - kiʔlawnaʔ   Ktunaxa - nupqu

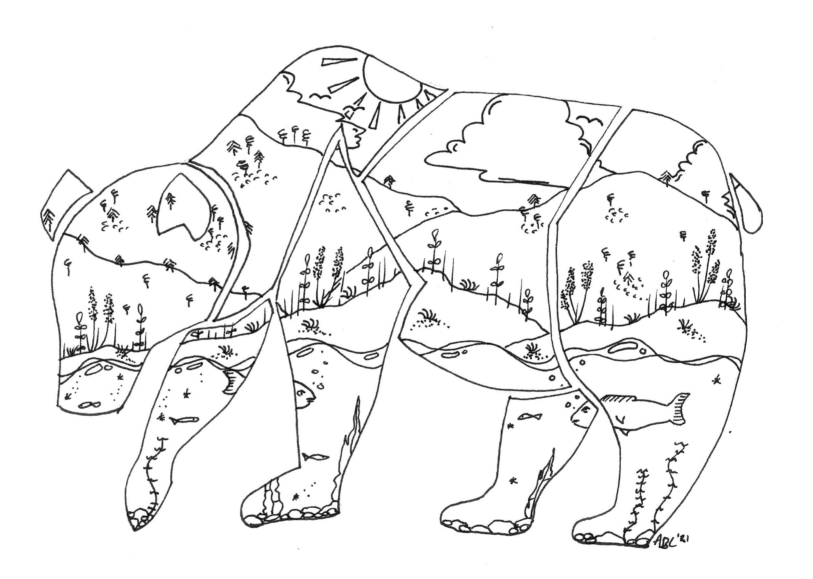

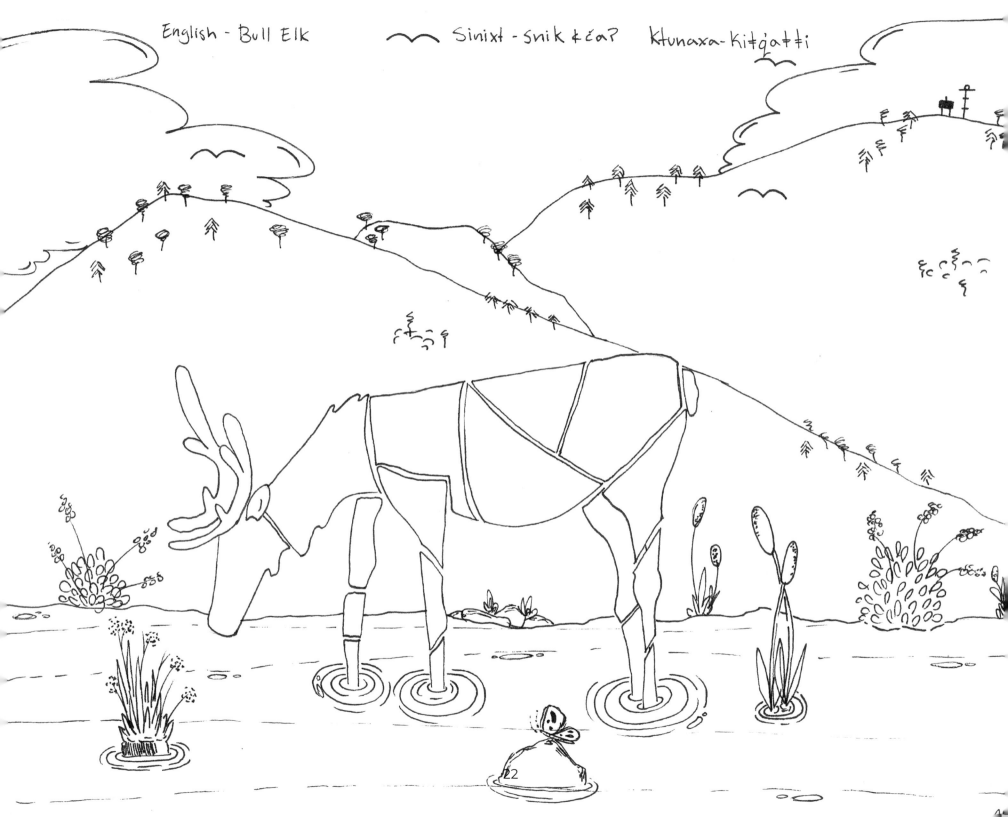

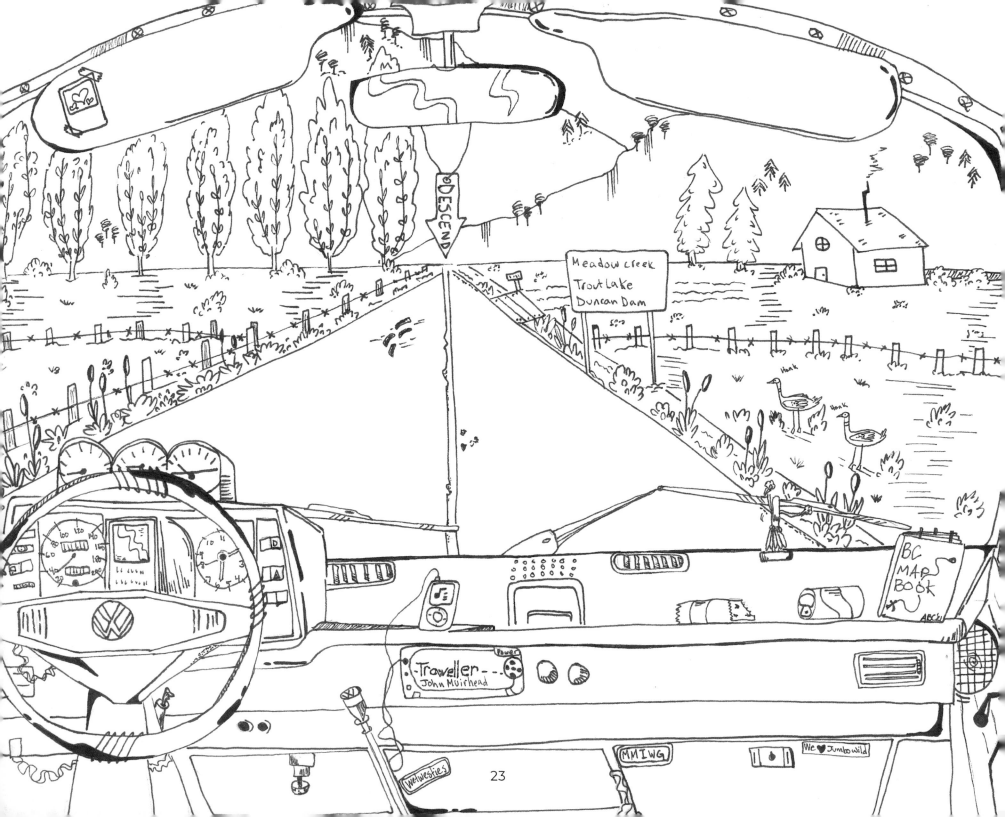

English - Eagle   Sinixt - miǝnups   Ktunaxa - Kyaq̓nuqa'ł

English - Idaho Peak

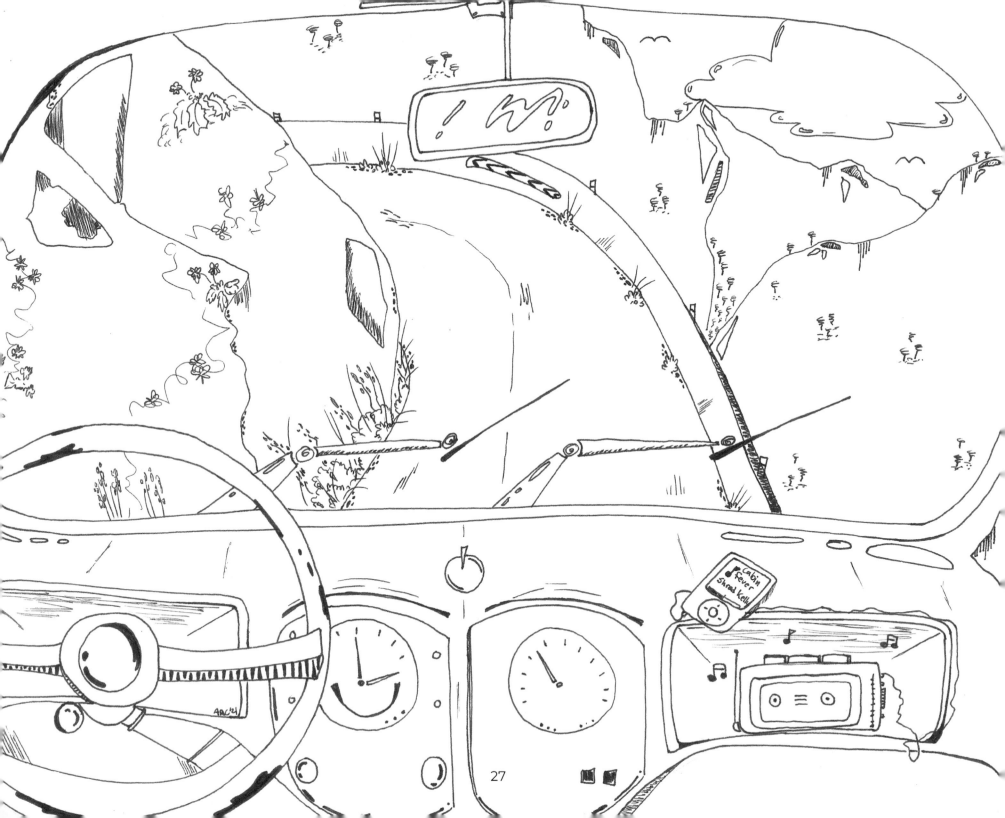

English - Jumbo Pass Ktunaxa - Qatmuk

English - Chicken
Ktunaxa - ȼikin

Glossary

- **Mentioned Artists and where to find them**
  John Muirhead - https://www.johnpmuirhead.com
  Shred Kelly - http://www.shredkelly.com
  Yundankasaurusrex - YouTube, SoundCloud
  Earth Freaks - Instagram

- **Info on how to save / support Jumbo Wild**
  https://www.patagonia.ca/stories/keep-jumbo-wild-the-fight-to-protect-jumbo-glacier/story-17649.html
  https://www.ecosociety.ca/campaign/keep-jumbo-wild/
  https://keepitwild.ca

- **Info on the REDDress Project / Moosehide Squares**
  https://www.jaimeblackartist.com/exhibitions/
  https://kumugwe.ca/red-dress-awareness-campaign/
  https://moosehidecampaign.ca

- **Resources to learn more**
  Salish school of Spokane - http://interiorsalish.com
  Yaqan Nukiy School - https://wwwyaqannukischool.org

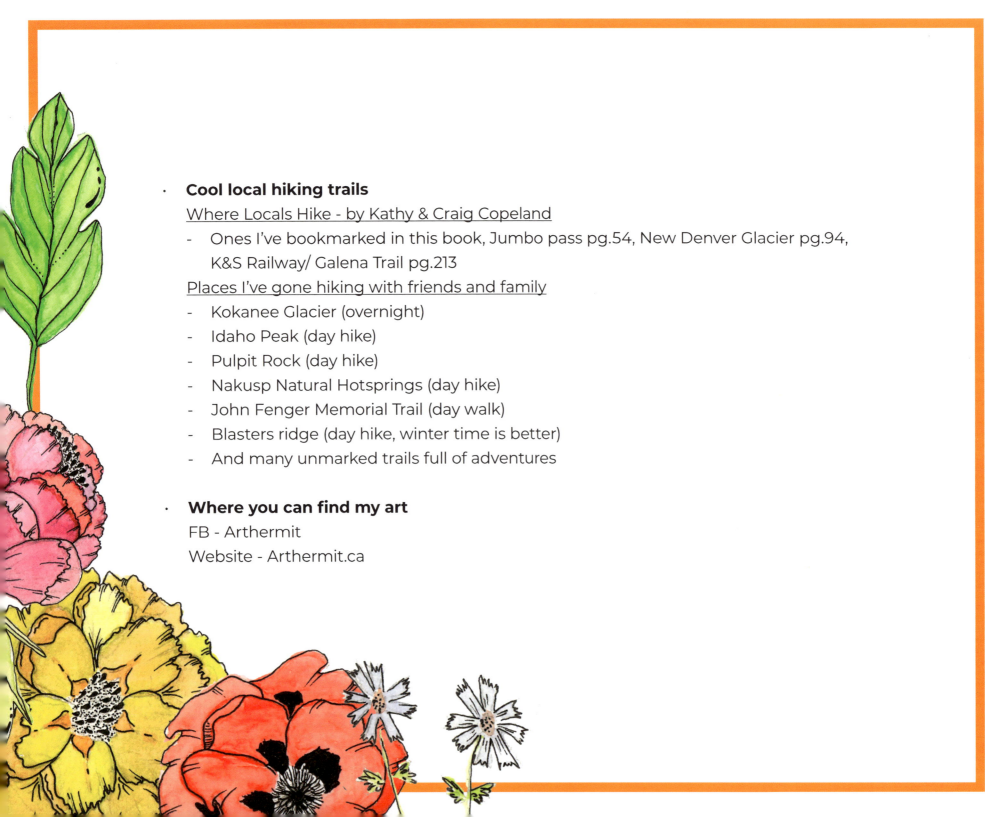

- **Cool local hiking trails**

  <u>Where Locals Hike - by Kathy & Craig Copeland</u>
  - Ones I've bookmarked in this book, Jumbo pass pg.54, New Denver Glacier pg.94, K&S Railway/ Galena Trail pg.213

  <u>Places I've gone hiking with friends and family</u>
  - Kokanee Glacier (overnight)
  - Idaho Peak (day hike)
  - Pulpit Rock (day hike)
  - Nakusp Natural Hotsprings (day hike)
  - John Fenger Memorial Trail (day walk)
  - Blasters ridge (day hike, winter time is better)
  - And many unmarked trails full of adventures

- **Where you can find my art**

  FB - Arthermit
  Website - Arthermit.ca